# Dangerous Rumors

R. E. Toresen

Photos by Bob Langrish

# Dangerous Rumors

R. E. Toresen

# The main characters:

Kimberly

Rebecca

Enrique

Paulina

Julio

San Silvo

Duquesa

Evel

# Chapter 1

"This is just like a dream. No – it's ten thousand times better than a dream – this is for real!" I turned to my friend Rebecca. If my ears hadn't blocked the way, I'm sure my smile would have stretched right around my head. "Just think about it; yesterday morning I was at home in Vermont. Sleet was pelting down, and the wind was freezing cold, and now I'm here. The sun is shining, and it's so hot I don't even need a sweater. You're so lucky living here in Portugal!"

I leaned forward to pat Evel, the beautiful gray horse that would be my ride for the whole spring break. Evel snorted softly and nodded his head, as if to say that he was quite pleased with his unfamiliar rider.

Little more than an hour had passed since I'd mounted him for the first time. I was more than a little nervous at first. My heart beat fast and my hands were all sweaty. He was so tall compared to what I was used to. At home, at the local riding school, I'd only been riding ponies. They were so docile and dependable that sitting on their backs was boring, even for an inexperienced rider like me. A thoroughbred Lusitano was something else altogether. It was not only his height that intimidated me. What if he was so hot-blooded and high-strung that I couldn't control him?

Apparently I needn't have worried. Evel seemed calm and well tempered, so after about five minutes I had slowly begun to relax and enjoy the ride. He was a great mount, with a soft, springy gait that carried me safely through the lush green landscape.

"What a stroke of luck that your dad had to come to Lisbon on business this week and was able to accompany you," Rebecca said happily. "Or do you think your parents would have let you travel alone?"

I shook my head. "Never! Well, Dad might have let me, but Mom would have had a fit at the thought of me being alone in the big wide world. You know how she is, seeing imaginary dangers around every bend. I mean, just think about it, what could possibly happen to me on a direct flight to Lisbon? Nothing! But try telling my mom that. She'd be afraid that the plane would be hijacked or have to make an emergency landing somewhere. For the first time in my life I'm glad Dad travels a lot in his job."

Rebecca Cortez and I are second cousins. She is half American and half Portuguese. Her dad and my mom were cousins. From kindergarten to fourth grade, Rebecca and I were best friends and next-door neighbors. Then her dad was killed in a tragic and senseless car accident. I can still remember the shock and the numb feeling when it happened. It took a long time, especially for Rebecca, to come to terms with the fact that her father was really gone forever.

A few months after the accident Paulina, Rebecca's mom, realized that she couldn't go on living in the family home, just her and Rebecca. So she moved back to Portugal. Since then Rebecca and I have only been able to meet once a year. We E-mail each other all the time, but it's not the same as being neighbors and getting together every day.

This was the first time I had come to stay with Rebecca on my own, and it was the very first time I had visited her in her new home – Quinta do Paraiso Alto, the stud farm Paulina had inherited from an uncle just six months earlier. The relocation had come quite unexpectedly, because Paulina had no idea that her uncle planned to leave his stud farm to her. He certainly knew what he was doing, I thought to myself. He couldn't have found anyone better suited for taking care of his horses.

"I'm so jealous," I sighed and looked around me. "You get to live in this fantastic place, surrounded by all the beautiful Lusitano horses!"

"Yes, it's a great place all right, but owning a stud farm is no bed of roses, I can tell you. At times it's really hard coping with everything. You just ask Mom!"

"Really? But I thought she loved it here . . . the land, the horses, everything. When she E-mailed Mom a few days ago, she seemed very happy and content with her new life."

Rebecca slowed her horse, Duquesa, to a standstill. She didn't say anything for a while. She just sat on the mare, stroking the soft, glistening mane, a serious, far-away expression on her face. Watching her I felt a stab of worry. Something was obviously worrying her. Could Paulina be sick or something?

"It's kind of hard to pinpoint what's wrong," Rebecca said at last. "But I have this creepy, uneasy feel-ing that something really unpleasant is going to happen any time now."

"Something unpleasant? What do you mean?" I looked at her ques-tioningly.

Rebecca shrugged. "I'm not sure what I mean," she said, urging Duquesa to start walking again. "Maybe I'm just let-ting my imagination run away with me. Or maybe it's because of all the trouble Mom's had

with our horrible neighbor . . . I don't know. I just have this awful, inner feeling of doom. Mom has been looking very worried lately, and it's not like her at all. She was so thrilled when we moved here, and so was I, but now . . ." Rebecca made a face and fell silent. We rode on for a while without speaking. When we turned onto the gravel road that led back to the farm, I finally spoke up. What she had said about her neighbor made me curious.

"Who is this horrible neighbor of yours and what's the problem?"

"Well, he hasn't given us any real difficulty so far, he's just so nasty and persistent. He shows up all the time, pestering Mom about San Silvo. Mom is really fed up, but there seems to be no stopping him."

San Silvo was the prize stallion at the stud, this much I knew. But what did the horse have to do with Rebecca's neighbor? Did San Silvo sneak into his vegetable garden in the middle of the night and eat his lettuce and carrots?

I was just about to ask when the roar from a car engine split the air. The next minute a small blue car, covered in dust, came hurtling down the road. It was heading straight at us. I expected the driver to slow down when he saw Rebecca and me, but he didn't. If anything, he seemed to increase his speed.

"Look out!" I shouted at Rebecca. "That madman is going to run us down!"

I dug my heels into Evel's flanks and steered him onto the grassy side of the road. Rebecca followed on his heels. It was a close call. The car sped past us with only inches to spare. I caught a brief glimpse of the driver. This was not some kid joyriding. It was a grown-up man. He didn't so much as glance at us when his car thundered by, so close that I could feel a rush of air following in its wake. The man behind the wheel kept staring straight ahead, a grim expression on his face. Evel disliked this blue noisy thing that roared past him, too close for comfort. He gave a protesting whinny and tossed his head. For a few nerve-wrecking moments I thought he would rear and throw me off, but to my relief, he calmed down as soon as the car had passed.

"That was way too close for comfort!" I said. My heart was hammering like crazy and my hands were shaking. "He didn't even slow down, and he had to have seen us. What was he thinking? We ought to report him to the police for driving like a lunatic. Do you know him?"

Rebecca nodded, her face paper white. "That's the man I told you about," she said. "He's our neighbor, Julio Merlota."

I turned in the saddle to look at the disappearing car. It sped into a curve and I held my breath. The car was going so fast it seemed impossible that it could cling to the road. I almost wished this Julio Merlota would end up in a ditch. It would serve him right for scaring us so, I thought vengefully. Somehow he managed to maneuver through the bend, and the next instant the car was out of sight.

"Come on, " Rebecca said, steering Duquesa back onto the road. "I bet he's been pestering Mom again. Let's hurry home and see if she's all right."

I had a thousand questions, but they would just have to wait. Rebecca was already cantering toward the farm and there was nothing for me to do but follow her.

What was wrong with this Mr. Merlota? Why was he behaving like he'd lost his mind? I gave this some thought while Evel stretched his legs, trying his best to catch up with Duquesa. I didn't have a clue about what was going on, but after the scary encounter with the blue car, I knew it had to be something far more serious than a quarrel about San Silvo feasting on Julio Merlota's vegetables.

Paulina heard the horses approaching and came out to meet us. Her face was hot and flushed, and she looked like she was on the verge of exploding. I knew she had a hot temper when she got really angry. Luckily that didn't happen very often. But her expression now made me remember something that had happened when Rebecca and I were about seven years old. We had arranged a tea party for our dolls, and Rebecca sneaked into the living room and "borrowed" the beautiful china teapot that Paulina had inherited from her great grandma. That Rebecca had been strictly forbidden to touch the teapot, had been momentarily forgotten. To make a long story short, we accidentally broke the teapot. Paulina was livid. The pot was the only thing she

had from her great grandma, so she was terribly upset and sad. I don't need to say that this was the last time Rebecca ever borrowed any of Paulina's things without permission.

Now Paulina was wearing the same expression that I remembered from all those years ago, but luckily, this time her anger was not directed at Rebecca and me.

"What happened?" Rebecca asked. "Mr. Merlota came down the road like the devil himself was after him. He almost ran us down. Kimberly and I barely managed to get out of his way!"

"He threatened me!" Paulina exclaimed. "Would you believe it? That horrible man had the nerve to threaten me in my own yard!" She looked incredulous as well as angry.

"How did he threaten you?" Now I was not only curious, but also worried. If Mr. Merlota was even half as crazy as he looked when he drove straight at us, he could very easily be dangerous. Just thinking about how close he had come to hitting us, made me shiver.

"Oh, it's a long story." Paulina sighed. "Ever since I took over the stud farm, he's been trying to talk me into selling San Silvo to him. It bugs him that I, a woman, am the owner of such a valuable prize stallion. He thinks that San Silvo should belong to him. He even tried to bluff me with some story about my uncle having promised to sell the stallion to him. Does he think I'm a complete idiot? I didn't believe him for a minute!"

Paulina sniffed disdainfully. "His stud farm is not going well, and that's an understatement, so I can understand why he's looking for a better stallion. But he will have to go look somewhere else and stop pestering me. That's what I told him."

She ran her hand through her short dark hair before continuing. "I can't believe why he would think I'd ever consider selling my prize stallion. San Silvo is the very foundation of running this business. Of course, we have some very promising colts here, but at the moment San Silvo is the star of the Quinta do Paraiso Alto. As well as using him to service our own brood mares, people from the region pay good money to have him sire their foals. I told Mr. Merlota that San Silvo wasn't for sale at any price. That's when he started threatening me. Paulina shook her head, as if she still found it hard to believe what happened.

"What did he say?" Rebecca asked.

"That I shouldn't be so cocky. He was going to win, one way or another. He'd soon teach me that it didn't pay to cross him. I told him to clear off and never show his face here again. That's when he jumped into his car and took off, livid. When I think about how easily he could have hurt you . . . Maybe I should phone the police and report the whole incident." Paulina considered this for a while, then she shrugged and said, "There's probably no point. He'll just deny everything and claim that we made it all up. I think we're better off trying to forget it. After all, nobody did get hurt."

"You should have seen him, Mom! He looked completely mad. Do you think he'll try to do anything else to hurt us?" Rebecca looked at her mom, a worried expression on her face.

Paulina shook her head. "I don't think so. I'm sure it's just empty threats on his part."

"But what if he kidnaps San Silvo?" Rebecca was not convinced.

Paulina laughed. "That would be a ridiculous thing for him to do. He knows he would be the prime suspect should San Silvo disappear. And he wouldn't be able to use a stolen horse for breeding. He'd be forced to keep the stallion's name a secret; which would kind of ruin the point, don't you think? He wouldn't make any money on an anonymous stallion. Don't worry, darling. There's nothing he can do to harm us. He's nothing but hot air, I'm sure. I just hope he has enough common sense to stay away from here. If not, he's going to be the sorry one. I'll make sure of that!" Paulina looked angry again. Then she glanced at her wristwatch, and with a startled exclamation that she was late for an appointment, she was gone.

While we groomed our horses, Rebecca told me a bit more about Julio Merlota. He had bought his stud farm two years ago, with big plans of becoming rich and powerful in a hurry.

"But the horses he bought can't compete with ours when it comes to quality," Rebecca said, brushing Duquesa's back with long, even strokes. Duquesa seemed to enjoy the treatment to the full. She and Evel stood facing each other, both looking happy and relaxed. They were so cute. Just watching the two best friends gave me a warm feeling inside.

"It seems to bother Mr. Merlota no end that Mom is more successful than he is," Rebecca said, shaking her head. "He's terribly old-fashioned and apparently thinks that a woman should be sweet and obedient and leave business to men. Is he stupid or what? It proves how little he knows about Mom, that's for sure!"

I giggled, trying to envision Paulina being sweet and obedient. The picture just wouldn't form. Paulina can be very sweet and kind, but when the going gets tough, she gets tougher. As for business, she has a better knowledge of it than your average person. Before moving back to Portugal she was head of the accounts department in a big company. No doubt she was much better suited for running a successful business than Mr. Merlota would ever be, I thought gleefully.

"If he were smart, he'd propose to your mom instead of threatening her," I quipped. "They could make the two stud farms into one and be rich and famous."

"You can't be serious!" Rebecca stuck out her tongue at me. "Would you like to have a creep like that for a stepfather? Thanks, but no thanks! I don't even think he's treating his horses very well. At least, I've heard some rumors to that effect."

"Calm down, I was just kidding!" I laughed and dodged Rebecca's attempt to throw her grooming brush at me.

"Hi, what are you two up to?" The deep voice that came from behind startled me. I turned around and froze. Had my heart been beating fast earlier, it now felt like it was going to jump right out of my chest. For one horrible second I thought Julio Merlota was standing there. But then I realized it wasn't him. This man was much younger. In fact, he looked no more than eighteen, twenty tops. My heart slowed down, but only a little. He was startlingly handsome with a nice friendly smile. What a pity he isn't a bit younger, I thought, while Rebecca said, "Hi, Enrique! We're not doing anything special, just grooming the horses. This is my cousin, Kimberly Howard. She's the one I told you about the other day."

"Hi Kimberly, welcome to Quinta do Paraiso Alto," Enrique said, shaking my hand. He had a good, firm shake and seemed very nice. "I'm Enrique Sandor. I've been working here at the stud farm for two months now."

He grinned at me, and my heart did its jump-out-of-the-chest thing again.

"I was supposed to be studying computer technology," he continued, "but suddenly

I got totally fed up with my studies, so I decided to take a year off, doing something completely different. I asked around, and when I heard help was needed here, I applied and got the job. And I haven't regretted it yet." Another dazzling smile, and I felt my face turn crimson. I hoped he and Rebecca would think I was flushed from the heat of the sun. I knew that Rebecca would tease me mercilessly if she discovered the effect Enrique had on me.

"Enrique is so good with the horses," Rebecca enthused, looking at him with open admiration. "Mom says her life has become so much easier with you here to help out. She doesn't know what she'd do without you."

"She really said that? That was nice of her." Enrique looked pleased and flattered. "I struck gold when I landed this job. Who could ask for more? I have my own living quarters right here on the property and I get to work with these beautiful horses every day. Maybe I won't go back to my studies. I might get my own stud farm one day. At the moment it seems far more appealing than staring into a computer screen all of the time."

"Or you could chase off Julio Merlota and take over his stud farm," Rebecca suggested, a mischievous smile on her face. "Kimberly and I were just talking about that awful man. He was here again today, and this time he threatened my mom."

"What?" Enrique's smile disappeared. "That guy's too much. What's wrong with him, anyway? Why can't he just give up and leave Paulina alone? He's making such a fool of himself."

"Maybe he thinks he can scare Mom into selling the Quinta do Paraiso Alto." Rebecca replied. "Well, he can think again! Mom won't let a creep like that intimidate her, no matter how unpleasant he is!"

"That's for sure. Paulina's great!" Enrique said admiringly.

We talked some more, and then Enrique said good-bye and went to the stables to get on with his chores. Watching him as he walked away, I sighed wistfully. Oh, why couldn't he have been just a bit younger, let's say fifteen? But he wasn't, so there was no use in wishing for the impossible. I sighed again and turned my attention to Evel. While grooming him, my thoughts kept straying to Julio Merlota. Rebecca and Paulina both seemed convinced that his threats were empty. I hoped they were right. They ought to know; they knew him better than I did. But I was afraid that he wouldn't give up so easily. And now, along with Rebecca's strange feeling of doom and gloom, I had an uneasy feeling that we hadn't seen the last of Julio Merlota yet.

# Chapter 2

I was riding on soft green grass through a beautiful orange grove. The sun was shining brilliantly from a clear blue sky, and everything was nice and peaceful. Evel was running at a steady canter and I relished the soft summer breeze on my face. Could life be any better than this? I turned my head to say something to Rebecca, but she was gone. How was that possible? She'd been there just a minute ago. Now the orange grove was gone as well. What was happening? Ahead of me was a belt of tall, withered trees that looked hostile and forbidding. Then the track suddenly forked in all directions, just as a horse whinnied in distress somewhere behind the trees. The horse was in danger . . . terrible danger. I had to choose the right path and save the poor animal from some cruel destiny. But which track was the right one? The sound seemed to come from all directions at once. Soon, very soon, it would be too late. In a moment the horse would be . . .

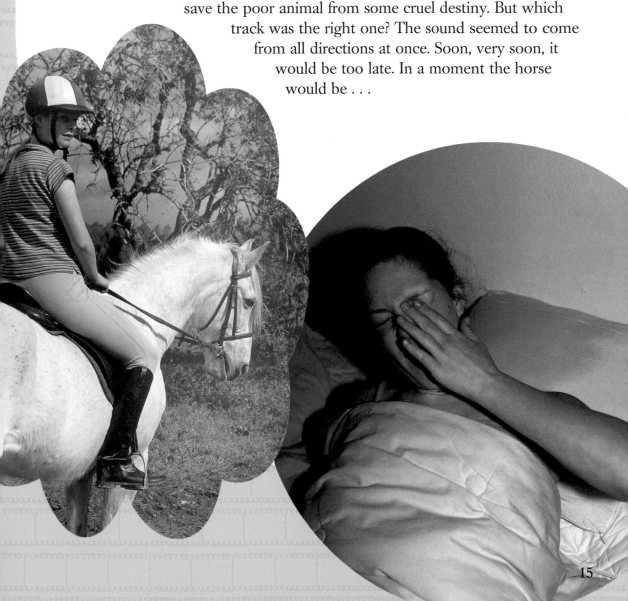

I woke up with a start and sat upright in bed. It was still nighttime – dark and quiet. Thank goodness it had all been a dream. I sank back into my pillow with a sigh of relief. Just as I was drifting off to sleep again, I thought I heard the whinnies again. I sat up and strained my ears. Had the sound come from the stables? I sat there listening for a long time, but heard nothing more. In the end I thought it must have been in my mind, probably some "echo" of my scary dream. I plunked down again, wrapped the down blanket around me, and was asleep almost immediately, happily unaware of the drama taking place in the stables just then.

Rebecca and I were sitting at the breakfast table when Paulina came storming into the kitchen. Without taking time to say good morning, she exclaimed, "There's total chaos in the stables. San Silvo went berserk last night. He kicked his stall door to pieces and ran completely wild afterward. He was soaked in sweat when Enrique came in this morning. It's a miracle the horse wasn't hurt. I can't even begin to imagine what made him panic like that. I've phoned the vet. He should be here any minute now. San Silvo must be sick. I have never ever experienced anything like this before!"

Paulina rushed out again without giving us a chance to say anything at all. Rebecca and I looked at each other, shocked. Suddenly I remembered the dream I'd had. Was part of it real? When I thought I heard a horse whinnying for help, could that have been San Silvo?

"I hope there is nothing serious wrong with San Silvo," Rebecca said worriedly and got up from the table. "Mom's right. It isn't like him at all to behave like that. Come on, Kimberly, let's go out to the stables and see what's happening. Maybe the vet is there by now."

We were about to enter the stables when Enrique came out and stopped us. "Sorry, girls, you can't go in there now," he said, his expression grave. "The vet is with San Silvo, checking him out. We'd better leave them alone. We don't want to make San Silvo more upset than he is already."

Rebecca looked like she wanted to protest, but then she realized that Enrique was right. We hung around the stables waiting impatiently for the vet to come out. It seemed like hours had passed before he finally appeared. Enrique hurried over to him and they had a brief conversation. Then the vet left in his car, and Enrique came back to us.

"Good news!" he said. "The vet didn't find anything wrong with San Silvo. He thinks that something must have scared the horse. Maybe rats or something like that."

"But we don't have rats at the stables," Rebecca protested indignantly.

Enrique shrugged. "I'm just repeating what the vet said. It could have been something other than rats that spooked San Silvo. What it was, we may never know. But it's obvious that something totally terrified the poor animal."

Enrique put his hands in his pockets as if he felt cold. I've never seen a horse in such a state before," he said. "It was frightening. There was froth around his muzzle and the whites of his eyes were showing. He was completely crazed. The vet gave him a sedative, so he should be better now. I just wish we knew what it was that scared him so."

In my head I suddenly envisioned a pack of huge fat rats. Their long, pink hairless tails were trailing after them

while they ran in circles around a panicky San Silvo. Red eyes glittering in anticipation, they bared their small, pointed teeth. I shivered. If there were rats in the stables, I would stay away from there. I can't stand rats. The only creatures that are more repulsive are huge hairy spiders.

I came back to reality with a start when Paulina stuck her head out the door and informed us that San Silvo was totally calm now. "But I'm going to stay with him for a while, just to be on the safe side," she said. "Even though the attack or whatever it was seems to be over now, I'm not taking any chances.

"Later today I'm going to call the Rodent Control," she added as an afterthought. "It's strange, though, we've never had rats here before. I guess there's a first time for everything." She shrugged and retreated to the stables.

There was no point in hanging around any longer, so Rebecca and I decided to go for a ride. We hurried to make our horses ready, called good-bye to Enrique, and then we were off.

The day was lovely, just perfect for a trail ride. The horses seemed alert and eager. Apparently, San Silvo's night riot had not disturbed their beauty sleep. Rebecca chose

a track that led us through lush green countryside. For a while we rode alongside a gurgling creek and we let our horses have a taste of the cool, fresh water. The ride should have been great, but neither Rebecca nor I was able to completely relax and enjoy it. The episode with San Silvo haunted both of us, and over and over again we talked about what could have frightened him so. But the discussions led us nowhere closer to finding out.

For a while we rode on without speaking. Then Rebecca said, "It's such a relief that Enrique is there to help Mom now. When she was handling all the work alone, it was really hard on her. I helped out with the stable chores, of course, but with school and everything there was only so much I could manage to do. Mom says that Enrique is a gem. He's a natural when it comes to handling the horses. Not to mention that he's a really nice guy."

"And good-looking!" I added with emphasis.

Rebecca giggled. "I'm glad he's way too old for you," she said. "Otherwise you two would probably be holding hands by now, gazing into each others eyes and forgetting all about me. I would have to go for rides all by myself and . . ."

"Knock it off!" I said, laughing. "I'd choose you and the horses before any boy, no matter how cute he is."

"That's more like it!" Rebecca grinned.

"By the way, have you noticed we've got company?" I said, pointing my thumb at a small dog that was trailing happily behind us, tail wagging.

"Oh, that's just Figaro. He belongs on one of the farms here," Rebecca said. "He always does this. He seems to enjoy following the horses, but after a while he gets bored and goes home. The horses are so used to him that they don't take notice of him anymore."

We rode on in silence for a while. My thoughts returned to San Silvo and his odd behavior. Suddenly something struck me. Why hadn't I thought of it before?

What if it wasn't rats that had scared the stallion? What if there had been thieves in the stables? Or even Mr. Merlota. He could easily have sneaked in to steal the valuable horse only to give up because San Silvo panicked so badly.

But the more I thought about my theory, the less likely it seemed. I remembered what Paulina said when Rebecca was afraid Mr. Merlota would kidnap San Silvo. A well-known stallion like this would be useless to anyone in the district. If Merlota planned to steal him, he would have to take the horse abroad. It was a long drive to the border, so he'd probably be stopped and arrested before he got there.

"Do you see the buildings over there?" Rebecca's voice interrupted my thoughts. She pointed toward a farm on the right side of the road. "That's Mr. Merlota's stud farm. I'm grateful we have so much land that we can't see his house from home. Just the thought of Julio Merlota gives me the creeps. He's the most unpleasant person I've ever met. I wish he'd take all his horses and disappear, preferably to another planet!"

"In your dreams," I started to say, but just then a loud bang sounded close by. The unexpected noise startled poor Evel. He let out a long, shrill whinny and jumped sideways, as if he was trying to get away from the scary sound. I had been sitting on his back, totally relaxed, and I was definitely not prepared for this, so I didn't stand a chance. I flew from the saddle and landed with a thud on the ground. I lay there for several seconds, winded and confused, and not able to move. I could just watch helplessly when Evel, completely in the grip of panic now, took off at a gallop.

"Stop him!" I gasped, but it wasn't necessary. Rebecca had already turned Duquesa and was in hot pursuit of the runaway.

Slowly I sat up and rubbed my shoulder. Ouch – that hurt! The pain brought tears to my eyes. Was it broken? Gingerly, I moved my arm, wincing as a fresh stab of pain shot through my body. But soon it subsided to a dull throb and I was pretty sure that my shoulder was just bruised. Thank goodness for small mercies, I thought. My hip hurt as well, but not as badly as my shoulder. While I sat there feeling sorry for myself, I heard the dry snap of a twig somewhere close by. Was someone there? Had they seen me fall? How humiliating!

Slowly I turned my head, then froze. By the fence at the roadside a man stood watching me. He held something in his hand. At first I didn't realize what it was, but then I saw it was a gun. Only then did it occur to me that the sound that scared Evel out of his wits had been a gunshot. I recognized the man immediately, even though I'd only seen a glimpse of him before – yesterday, when he almost ran us down with his car. Julio Merlota! Had he shot at us on purpose? I felt nauseous with fright as the terrible truth dawned on me. I was alone here, with an armed and possibly crazy man standing just a few yards away.

If he points his gun at me, I'll die of shock. He won't need to shoot me, I thought hysterically. But Mr. Merlota didn't raise his gun. He just stared, long and hard, and then abruptly he turned and marched away toward his house without a backward glance.

Shakily I scrambled to my feet. Thundering heartbeats pounded in my ears and my legs felt strange, like they weren't mine at all and might give way any second. But they didn't fold; they somehow supported me, even though my knees felt like spaghetti.

As I stood there watching Mr. Merlota walk away, I felt a mixture of anger and relief. I was relieved that he hadn't hurt me, but at the same time I was angry because he hadn't even bothered to ask if I was okay after my fall. And had the gun-shot been an unfortunate coincidence, or had he fired his gun on purpose to scare us? But why would he want to do that? We hadn't done anything to make him angry.

Time passed incredibly slowly. It felt like I'd been waiting forever for Rebecca to return. What was taking her so long? Maybe she wasn't able to catch Evel – or maybe he was hurt. I was worried out of my mind when she finally appeared with Evel in tow. He looked perfectly sound. My relief was so strong that I had to fight to hold the tears back.

"Phew! What a chase he led me. I thought he was never going to stop! But finally I caught up with him, and here he is, safe and no worse for wear!"

Rebecca handed me Evel's reins and I clambered onto his back.

"I wonder what made the banging noise that sent him off in panic," Rebecca mused while we were heading home.

"I know what it was," I said and shuddered. Then I told her all about Mr. Merlota and his gun.

"Do you think he could have done it on purpose, just to frighten us?" I asked when I'd finished my story.

"He's such a hateful man, I wouldn't put it past him," Rebecca said worriedly.

"I guess we'd better tell Paulina about it," I suggested.

Rebecca nodded. "Definitely. Mom will be livid when she hears about this. Just you wait. She's going to jump straight into her car and go and give Mr. Merlota the telling-off of his life!"

Rebecca got that right. Paulina was furious. We hardly had time to finish our story before she was running to her car to go and give Mr. Merlota a piece of her mind.

Rebecca and I asked to come along. We didn't want to miss this. Now we were sitting in Paulina's car, listening to the shouting match of the century. But if we had expected Mr. Merlota to assume the role of repentant sinner, we were sadly disappointed.

"It was an accident, I tell you!" he yelled at the top of his lungs. "I had no idea those stupid girls were anywhere close! Why on earth would I want to scare them?"

Paulina said something I didn't catch, and then Mr. Merlota's voice filled the air again.

"I have the right to shoot vermin on my own property, so don't you come here and try to lecture me! When you send two clueless kids out on skittish horses that will shy at anything, you only have yourself to blame if something happens!"

With that Mr. Merlota just turned his back to Paulina and left. Paulina, for once at loss for words, just stood there staring at his rigid, angry back.

"The nerve of that man!" she said when she was back in the car. "Trying to put the blame on me!" She shook her head.

"But did you believe him when he said it was an accident?" Rebecca asked, looking at her mom.

Paulina hesitated for a minute, and then she nodded. "I guess I do," she said. "I really can't see what kind of motive he'd have for trying to hurt or scare the two of you. But even if it was an accident, he should have checked that Kimberly was okay, instead of just walking away. That's something I won't forget in a hurry, he can be sure of that!"

# Chapter 3

Rebecca and I didn't feel like riding out anymore that day, so after lunch we practiced dressage in one of the paddocks.

"This is kind of boring," Rebecca said after a while. "Maybe we could set up a few bars and practice jumping instead."

"Sounds like fun, but let's wait until tomorrow," I said, flexing my arms and wincing. "At the moment my shoulder isn't fit for anything but light and easy riding. Hopefully, it will be better tomorrow."

"Look, here comes Enrique with San Silvo," Rebecca exclaimed. "I think he's going to lunge the horse. Would you like to watch?"

I nodded eagerly. "I'd love to finally see the wonder horse in action," I said. "Come, on, let's tether our horses and go have a look. Do you think he'd let me try my hand with lunging San Silvo?"

"Of course. Just smile and bat your eyelashes at him, and he'll agree to anything." Rebecca giggled and ducked to avoid the sand I scooped up and threw at her.

After Rebecca's teasing I would never have had the nerve to ask Enrique about anything whatsoever, so we just stood at the edge of the course watching him work with the stallion.

"San Silvo seems perfectly okay now," Rebecca said, keeping her voice low. "He looks just as calm and collected as he usually does when he's working out. When I think about how easily he could have been hurt last night, I feel sick to my stomach."

"But he wasn't hurt," I said soothingly. "Let's just hope that no more rats or whatever it was, will bother him again."

"Hi girls," Enrique suddenly called. "Do you want to take over the lunging for a while? My arms are getting pretty tired."

"Oh, yes please!" I was at his side in a flash. Enrique showed me what to do, and I looked admiringly at the big horse that circled around me, his gait energetic and elegant. He was so beautiful that I felt tears sting my eyes. There is nothing more spectacular than a horse, I thought to myself, and glanced at Enrique. Well, there might be a boy or two that came close. Quickly, I looked away from him, feeling a serious blush coming on.

Enrique had taken over the lunge line again by the time Paulina joined us. She was so angry her entire body shook.

"A journalist from the local newspaper just called," she said. "He wanted to know if it's true that our prize stallion had lost his mind. Someone told him that San Silvo has been breaking out of his stall every night for ages and that he has attacked both people and other horses. Why on earth would anyone contact the newspaper to tell rubbish like this?"

"Ask Julio Merlota!" Rebecca said angrily. "I bet he's behind this. Remember, he told you he was going to make you sorry for turning down his offer."

"But how would he know we had a problem with San Silvo?" Paulina asked. "I most certainly didn't tell him!"

"Maybe the vet did," Enrique suggested. "He mentioned he was going to Mr. Merlota's place from here."

"But why would the vet go around telling people that the horse is crazy?" Paulina objected. Then she clasped a hand to her forehead. "Of course! How stupid of me! The vet probably told him the bare facts about what happened, and then Mr. Merlota added some juicy details on his own! I'm just grateful the journalist phoned me, so I could put him straight about what really happened. Imagine people's reaction had a story like that been published!"

"Why don't you call Mr. Merlota and ask him what he's up to," Rebecca suggested. She was so angry she was pacing back and forth, unable to keep still.

Paulina shook her head. "It's no use, he'll just deny it, and we don't really know that he's behind this, we just suspect he is."

She thought for a while, then said, "I think I'll ask the vet to come back tomorrow and check on San Silvo again. And afterward he can tell everyone that the horse is as fit as a fiddle. I'm sure that would put a stop to the silly rumor before it can spread.

It sounded like a good plan. The only problem was that even the best plan could fail. When Rebecca and I came down for breakfast the next morning, a very upset Paulina met us. She told us it had happened again – San Silvo had gone amok.

"The vet is with him now," Paulina said. "I have to go talk with him." She left the room before we had a chance to ask her any more questions.

The morning had a déjà vu quality to it and seemed endless. Once again Rebecca and I were banned from the stables, and every time we tried to ask Paulina or Enrique if San Silvo would be all right, they just shook their heads and refused to answer.

To try and make time go faster, Rebecca and I saddled and bridled our horses and rode in the paddock. I tried to concentrate on Evel and how well he was going for

me, but my thoughts were really in the stables with San Silvo. Why did it take so long? The vet had been there forever. When he finally emerged, followed by Paulina, Rebecca and I could hardly wait to hear what was happening. As soon as the vet drove away, Paulina came running toward us.

"How is he?" Rebecca and I asked simultaneously.

"Much better, thank heavens!" Paulina said. "But he needed a double dose of tranquilizers this time. He was in really bad shape, shaking like a leaf and soaked in sweat. When he finally calmed down, the vet checked him thoroughly without finding anything wrong. But there has to be something! He's not acting like this for nothing! And now that we know that it was definitely not rats that made him panic, we have to look for the cause elsewhere."

I knew that three men from the Rodent Control had done a thorough search through the stables yesterday without finding a trace of even the tiniest little mouse...

Paulina combed her fingers through her hair and sighed. "I'm going to take San Silvo to the veterinary college later today and have his brain scanned, just to be on the safe side."

I felt a cold shiver run down my spine. A brain scan! Could he have a brain tumor or something like that? It would certainly explain his strange behavior. But a tumor could kill San Silvo! Just thinking that the beautiful horse might die made my stomach clench. Please, no! Don't let it be true, I prayed. There's got to be another reason for what's happening to him!

"Let's hope there's nothing wrong," Paulina went on, "but to be honest, I'm worried. San Silvo has never been even remotely nervous before. His behavior now is totally out of character."

Rebecca and I looked at one another. We didn't know what to say.

"I should go back to San Silvo," Paulina said. "Enrique is with him now, but I know he's got a lot on his plate today, so I better let him get on with his work." She hesitated a moment, then continued, "The vet was acting really strange today. He's usually such a nice friendly guy, but this morning he was abrupt and kind of standoffish. I got the impression that he thinks what's happening to San Silvo is my fault somehow."

"But how could it be?" Rebecca looked uncomprehendingly at her mom. "You've done all you can to find out what's upsetting San Silvo. I'm sure the vet knows that."

"You're probably right." Paulina shrugged. "I'm letting my imagination run wild. Maybe because I'm so upset about what's happening. Enough. Let's not panic until we have to. There must be some logical explanation to all of this. In my heart of hearts, I don't really believe that San Silvo can be seriously sick . . ."

Her voice trailed away, as if she hadn't even succeeded in convincing herself. I watched her head toward the stables, suddenly looking small and fragile. I felt a big lump in my throat. Please, oh please, let San Silvo be okay, I prayed silently. Let this be the end of our problems. But deep down I didn't believe this was the end for a minute. I had an uneasy feeling that it was the beginning – the start of worse trouble to come.

# Chapter 4

"Let's not talk about San Silvo for a while," Rebecca said firmly. "It doesn't help at all. The more we discuss what's wrong, the worse I feel."

"I guess you're right," I agreed. "But it's almost impossible to think about anything else."

We had been out riding for an hour or so, talking nonstop about the troubled stallion and what could be wrong with him.

"I know what we could do! Race each other!" Rebecca grinned, obviously pleased with her own idea.

"Sounds like a plan to me!" I said, looking around me. The riding track was wide, with a soft surface. It would be perfect for a canter. "How far should we go?"

"There's an old barn down the track from here," Rebecca said. "What do you say we race to it?"

"You're on! And the loser is rotten egg!" I adjusted my position in the saddle, collected my reins and off Evel and I went.

"You'll be the rotten egg!" Rebecca shouted after me. "You're a cheater, you jumped the gun! But it won't help you. Duquesa is faster than greased lightning!"

I didn't reply. I was concentrating on sitting correctly in the saddle, not tugging at the reins. I didn't want to slow Evel down. It was easy to see that he enjoyed his canter. He went forward like a rocket, without my having to urge him on.

But Duquesa was faster. The sound of hoofbeats from behind told me that Rebecca was gaining on Evel and me. But not fast enough. We still had a fair chance of keeping them at bay. The soft breeze felt wonderful on my hot face and I laughed out loud from pure joy. The speed made my eyes water. This was fantastic!

"Evel, you're the best horse in the whole wide world," I told him excitedly.

Just then a scream from behind us made me start. What the . . .? For a minute I thought that Rebecca had screamed to try and trick me into slowing down, so that she and Duquesa could overtake us. But a quick glimpse over my shoulder told me that this was not the case.

For some reason Duquesa had reared. Just as I turned to look, she landed on all four legs again and stopped short. She seemed very agitated, and trotted on the spot, as if debating – should I stay or should I run away? Luckily, she decided to stay, because there was no one up top who could have stopped her. Her saddle was very empty. Rebecca was lying on the ground, clutching her face and moaning softly.

I turned Evel as fast as I could and rode back to where Rebecca was still on the ground. She sat up just as I approached her.

"What happened?" I said worriedly. "Are you hurt?"

"My head hit a rock or something!" Rebecca whimpered, trailing her hand across her bruised face. "I'm going to have a black eye, that's for sure. It's already swollen, and it's throbbing like mad."

"Good thing you had your riding cap on, or this would have been far more serious." I gave her a long hard look. "Are you sure your eye is the only thing hurting?"

Rebecca nodded and scrambled to her feet. "I feel okay, just a little shaky. I wonder what got into Duquesa? She was cantering as right as rain, and then, straight out of the blue, she reared up and threw me off. I didn't have a chance of staying in the saddle. She took me completely by surprise. But I've been thrown off in worse places than this." She nodded toward the soft heather covering the ground. "I wouldn't have been hurt at all if it wasn't for that stupid rock lying there in the middle of the heather."

"No wonder Duquesa reared," I said after examining the horse. "Look here! She's lost her left hind shoe. It's lying over there. She must have been spooked when it fell off."

"Just my luck!" Rebecca sighed. "The farrier was going to come by next week to check on Duquesa's hoofs. Why couldn't the stupid shoe have stayed in place until then? Why did it have to fall off just now?"

Rebecca stared bleakly at the abandoned horseshoe as if she suspected it of having fallen off just to spite her.

"Why don't you ask the shoe?" I said, my voice heavy with irony. "All kidding aside, what do we do now?"

"We have to lead the horses back home, and then we'll visit the farrier, Mr. Almero, and ask him if he can come today and fix Duquesa's shoes.

"Why don't you just phone him?" I suggested.

"No, I'd like to drop by. Mr. Almero is the local saddler as well, and I have some broken reins I want him to fix. This way we can kill two turds with one stone."

"Silly," I said, laughing. "That's birds, not turds! You've been living in Portugal too long. You don'ta speaka da proper Anglesa anymore!"

"Sounds like your English sucks more than mine!" Rebecca giggled. "And my Portuguese is better than yours!"

"You've got me there," I shrugged. "But it should be. You live here. I don't!" I turned to gather up Evel's reins. "Come on, boy," I said. "No more cantering for you today. Did you know that Duquesa is such a bad loser that she shed a shoe just to have an excuse for breaking off the race?"

"Hah! We were gaining on you big time," Rebecca snorted. "Just you wait until Duquesa has her new shoes. Then we'll show you!"


We were still in the middle of a friendly haggle about who had the fastest horse by the time we entered Mr. Almero's shop.

"Hi, Mr. Almero," Rebecca said. "Duquesa has lost a shoe. Is it possible for you to come by and fix it today? And I need these to be mended."

She held out the broken reins. Mr. Almero reached out his hand to take them, and then he froze, his friendly smile gone.

"Good heavens!" he exclaimed. "Don't tell me she's beating you, too!" His gaze was fixed at Rebecca's black eye.

Rebecca just looked at him, uncomprehending. "Beat me? Who? I don't know what you mean. Kimberly and I did not fight. I got this when I fell off my horse. Duquesa reared because she lost her shoe and I was thrown off and bumped my head on a rock."

"Oh . . . I'm sorry . . . I didn't realize . . ." Mr. Almero was clearly at a loss for words.

I looked at him curiously. Why had he jumped to the conclusion that I'd beaten Rebecca? Did I really look brutal?

Mr. Almero glanced at his wristwatch. "I have no appointments for two hours," he said. "It's a slow day in the shop. My assistant can handle things while I'm away. I'll go ahead and fix Duquesa's hoofs immediately, if you like."

He still regarded Rebecca with an odd, skeptical expression on his face.

What was going on here? Did he think that Rebecca was lying about the accident? I felt truly offended and humiliated.

"You can believe whatever you want, but you should know I'm not in the habit of beating up my friends!" My head held high, my back stiff with repressed fury, I marched toward the door.

"Wait! I didn't mean to . . ."

That's all I heard. The next minute I was outside, slamming the door behind me.

"He's really got a way with the horses. Just watch how calm Duquesa is when he's rasping her hoofs," Rebecca commented.

An hour had passed since we left Mr. Almero's shop. He was now in the process of cutting down Duquesa's hoofs to re-shoe her. Mr. Almero had brought his dogs, and they were running circles around Duquesa, sniffing at her legs. I had expected she would be upset and unsettled by their inquisitive noses, but she

didn't so much as blink an eye. Obviously, she was used to them.

"I don't care if he's got a million ways with horses," I grumbled, anger still ready to surface. "I don't like people who accuse me for no reason."

"No, that was a strange thing to do," Rebecca agreed. "I don't know why he would say a thing like that."

"And what did he mean by saying that I'd beaten you, too?" I continued. "Who else am I supposed to have beaten?"

"No idea." Rebecca shrugged. "I tried asking him after you'd stormed out of his shop, but he just started talking about something else. Maybe he mistook you for someone else and is embarrassed about it now."

"Then at least he could apologize," I mumbled, still annoyed.

"Let's just forget about him," Rebecca said, an impatient note in her voice. "Look, here comes Mom with the horse box. Oh, I hope she's going to tell us that San Silvo is all right."

Paulina jumped out of the car. She waved at us and hurried toward the house. "Help Enrique unload San Silvo," she called. "I just have to make a few phone calls. Enrique will tell you what happened."

But Enrique didn't need our help with San Silvo. When we reached the horsebox he'd already opened the doors and the stallion bounded out, snorting loudly, as if to say, "Finally, I get to move my legs again. Not a minute too soon!"

Enrique led him to one of the paddocks. After removing the travel bandages from San Silvo's legs and tail, he turned the stallion loose. San Silvo eagerly attacked the pile of hay that lay waiting for him on the ground.

"He looks like he's been starving for a week." Rebecca grinned. "He can't really

be sick with an appetite like that, can he?"

I watched the big, muscular horse. To me he looked like a beautiful animal in prime condition. It was hard to imagine anything was wrong with him.

Enrique went to the stables to put away the led rope and bandages. When he returned, Rebecca and I both looked at him expectantly.

"The scan didn't show anything abnormal," he said. "And they took lots of blood tests. Some of the results will take a few days, but all the rest showed normal values. The vet is fairly sure there's nothing physically wrong with San Silvo.

"But what's troubling him then?" There must be something!" Rebecca said.

Enrique merely shrugged. "I have no idea. I just hope we find out soon. There are already rumors going around . . ."

"What kind of rumors?" I asked him.

Enrique fidgeted and looked like he didn't want to answer, but then he sighed and said, "I guess I better tell you. You're only going to hear it from someone else, if I don't, the way tongues are wagging. Even at the clinic they'd heard the rumors."

He swallowed and went on. "People are saying that Paulina has ill-treated San Silvo so severely that the poor horse has lost his mind from all the whipping and beating."

I felt like someone had given me a hard punch to my stomach. I was so shocked that I found it hard to breathe normally.

"But nobody would believe such horrible things about Mom, would they?" Rebecca looked at Enrique pleadingly. "Mom loves the horses. She'd never beat them any more than she would beat me!"

As she said that, it came to me in a flash; this was what Mr. Almero had meant. He wasn't referring to me when he said, "Don't tell me she's beating you, too." He was talking about Paulina!

Suddenly I felt dizzy. This couldn't be true. Nobody in their right mind would believe that Paulina, who loved horses, was abusive to her animals. But according to Enrique, that was exactly what people thought. Not everybody, of course, but apparently quite a few.

"Paulina is phoning people she knows well," Enrique said. "We have to try and kill these stupid rumors before they have time to become "the truth". If they do, it will mean disaster to the stud farm. Nobody wants to do business with a horse tormenter!"

"But Mom is no horse tormenter!" Rebecca was on the verge of tears.

"I know that and you know that," Enrique said. "But most people don't. You've only lived here a short time and people don't know you very well. And when tongues start wagging . . ."

He broke off, frowning. "There must be something we can do. Yes! Maybe . . ." His somber expression lightened. "I think I have an idea," he said. "I'll run it by Paulina to hear what she thinks of it. Here she comes now. She must be finished phoning her friends."

Paulina seemed both indignant and resigned when she came up to us. "I've talked to the five friends that I trust most," she said. "They were shocked by the rumors and

promised to do anything they can to speak up for me, but I seriously doubt it will do any good."

"I think I know a way to stop this once and for all," Enrique said eagerly.

"We invite people to an Open House at the Quinta do Paraiso Alto. And the sooner the better. Preferably tomorrow."

"What would be the point of doing a thing like that?" Paulina was skeptical. "I fail to see how this would help."

"It's simple," Enrique said. "When people come here and see all the beautiful, well-groomed, even-tempered horses, they are going to realize that the rumors are not true. I could even do a demonstration of lunging San Silvo. Then people can see for themselves that the stallion is a normal calm horse and not a nervous ill-treated wreck."

Paulina considered this for a while, and then she nodded. "You know, this could actually work," she said. "And we have nothing to lose by trying. Will you help me phone all our friends and business associates who might be interested in coming?"

Enrique nodded. "Of course I will. Don't worry; this is going to work out fine. By tomorrow night, all your problems will be over."

I watched as they hurried toward the house. Would Enrique's plan be enough to stop the nasty rumors? I really hoped so, but what if something went wrong?

Rebecca had obviously been on the same wavelength. "I'm scared," she said. "What if San Silvo suddenly goes mad again right in front of everyone?"

"He won't," I said firmly, wishing I felt as confident as I sounded. "Enrique will have San Silvo under full control. Everything is going to go exactly as planned, and all the troubles will be over."

It sounded great, but the truth of it was that the problems would not be over until we knew who was behind the ugly rumors and why.

But one of the worst things about rumors is that it's very difficult to backtrack and find their source. Was Julio Merlota behind this? Would he really go this far just to get even? But . . . maybe this wasn't about revenge at all. Maybe this was his way of forcing Paulina so close to bankruptcy that she would have to sell San Silvo. Of course! Why hadn't I thought of this before? The difficulty would be in proving it, but I was determined to try. Tomorrow I would talk it over with Rebecca. Tomorrow, when the most immediate problems were over and the world hopefully looked brighter for Paulina.

# Chapter 5

"This has been the worst day of my life!" Rebecca's voice shook. She ran a hand through Duquesa's dark, silky mane and looked at me, tears in her eyes.

I knew exactly how she felt. The Open House day had been a failure. No, failure was an understatement. Disaster was more accurate.

In the beginning everything had gone as planned. I'd been amazed and impressed at how many people had showed up. Paulina and Enrique must have phoned half the district and everyone seemed to have come. Mr. Almero and the vet were the only familiar faces in the crowds that milled around the stables and paddocks. That is, until I went toward the house to find myself a cold soda. Suddenly I caught a glimpse of another familiar figure. Julio Merlota was standing by the fence outside one of the paddocks, watching two brood mares dozing lazily in the brilliant sunshine. When he saw me staring at him, he withdrew into the crowds and disappeared from sight. I didn't see him again, even though I kept looking for him. I felt a hard knot of rage in the pit of my stomach. The nerve of that man! Coming here to stroll around as if nothing had happened. Maybe he was hoping for some action. If so, he had no reason to feel disappointed. If he was still around when disaster struck, that is.

The atmosphere was positive and relaxed when Enrique brought San Silvo into an empty paddock. The big, beautiful stallion seemed to be in good spirits. He looked eager, but at the same time collected, ears pricked as he eyed his audience. The lunging went like a dream and I listened to people around me commenting on the horse. They talked about what a beauty he was, and how calm he appeared to be. They agreed that there seemed to be no truth in the rumors that he was supposed to be wild and dangerous.

I nudged Rebecca. "The plan is working even better than we hoped."

"Right. I don't think anybody believes those stupid rumors anymore. Maybe our troubles are over now," Rebecca said.

But just then it happened – the terri-

ble thing that wasn't supposed to happen. Enrique had finished his program and Paulina entered the paddock, pleased and smiling to praise horse and trainer. As she approached San Silvo, a shiver went through the horse's powerful body. The next instant his ears lay flat against his skull. He gave a piercing whinny, and then he reared up and flung himself sideways, eyes rolling in his head. The stallion looked terrified, as if evil itself in the shape of Paulina was coming to get him. Startled, Paulina backed away, but the harm was already done. The spectators got the distinct impression that San Silvo was so afraid of Paulina that just seeing her was enough to drive him crazy.

Paulina made a desperate attempt to tell everyone that there had to be another explanation to San Silvo's behavior, but of course, nobody listened to her. In their minds the answer was simple. The horse was terrified of Paulina; they had seen it with their own eyes.

Within two minutes we were alone in the stable yard. People had scattered and almost run to their cars, as if they were afraid Paulina would attack them if they stayed another second.

Paulina was devastated. "This is the end," she said, desperately. "I'm going to lose all my customers. What will I do? I'll probably have to sell the Quinta do Paraiso Alto."

She buried her face in her hands and burst into tears. "Everything I dreamed of just crumbled away. What's going on? Why is this happening to me? What have I done to deserve this?"

We had no good answers for her. For one horrible moment I wondered if there might be some truth in the rumors after all. Was it possible that Paulina could have done what they accused her of? The next minute I was so deeply ashamed of myself that I couldn't look at her. What was wrong with me? This was Paulina, whom I had known since I was born. She would never beat any living thing, I was sure of that. Even when she was livid with Rebecca and me all those years ago, I had not been afraid of her. I'd been sorry because we'd ruined her precious teapot, but not scared. I'd known instinctively that she'd never hurt me or anyone else.

A sound brought me back to the present. It came from Rebecca, who could no longer hold back her tears. She'd buried her face in Duquesa's mane, her body shaking with sobs. The mare just stood there, calm and patient, while Rebecca's tears spileed down her neck. I left Rebecca alone for a while, concentrating on patting Evel until I heard her voice behind me. It sounded hoarse, but firm.

"Kimberly, we have to do something to help Mom," she said, mopping her eyes. "She didn't do the awful things they accuse her of. Please say that you believe me!"

"Of course I do." I tried ignoring a sting of bad conscience. I had doubted Paulina. Only for a second or two, but still . . .

"Everything was fine until that awful Mr. Merlota started pestering Mom about selling San Silvo. Since then everything has gone wrong!" Rebecca reached for a tissue in her pocket and blew her nose with such a loud honk that Duquesa clipped her ears and looked at her questioningly.

Rebecca smiled and patted the mare's neck. "Relax," she said. "We don't need any more spooked

horses today. Didn't you ever hear anyone blow her nose before?"

Duquesa snorted, as if to say, "Well, if I did it was never this noisy!"

I had to laugh. She was so incredibly cute with her dark velvety eyes looking at us with such an innocent expression.

"You're right, we don't need any more frightened horses," I agreed. "So you and I will have to find out what's really going on here. It's definitely something fishy. Let's discuss it while we clean the saddles and bridles. Maybe we'll come up with some good ideas."

"Okay, I'll just run back to the house and change to a lighter sweater," Rebecca said, "before I have a complete melt-down!"

While Rebecca was gone I carried the saddles outside and fetched our grooming kits. Maybe we really will have a good idea, I told myself optimistically. I discovered long ago that my brain seems to work better when I'm busy doing something, rather than sitting at a desk trying to solve a math problem or whatever. Still, this was far more serious than your average math problem.

"By the way, you just said what I've been thinking about since yesterday," I told Rebecca when she was back and we were cleaning Evel's saddle.

"What was that?" Rebecca looked confused.

"That everything was fine until Julio Merlota came along and started hassling you.

I'm sure he's the one who started all those ugly rumors about Paulina, and I think he's behind what's happening to San Silvo as well."

"But how could he have anything to do with San Silvo?"

"Think about it," I said eagerly. "He wanted to buy the stallion, but Paulina said no. Even when he threatened her, she still wouldn't budge. Right afterward San Silvo started to act crazy in his stall. What if Mr. Merlota sneaked in there at night and scared the wits out of the horse? I have no idea how he did it, but it's possible, isn't it? You don't have an alarm system at the stables, and the lock on the door . . . well, even I could pick it without problem.

"You may be right!" Rebecca said eagerly. Then her shoulders slumped. "No, you can't be. Just think about what happened today. Mr. Merlota was nowhere close to San Silvo when he spooked."

"No, he wasn't," I said slowly, confused thoughts swirling through my brain, looking for a solution. Then suddenly, I found it. At least I thought I did. "If Mr. Merlota used an air gun or something like that, he wouldn't have to be close to San Silvo.

He could shoot something at the horse without anyone noticing. Didn't you see how San Silvo started just before he went wild?"

"But if it was Mr. Merlota, how are we going to prove it?" Rebecca looked at me. "So far he's been very slick and cunning. We don't have anything on him other than our suspicions."

"Then we have to find evidence, although I have no idea how," I said, scratching my forehead. "But it all fits so well. He wants San Silvo. I bet he's sitting at home right now, congratulating himself on his success, just waiting for Paulina to phone and offer him San Silvo on a silver platter.

"We have to find a way to keep him," Rebecca said. "But right now my head is totally empty. I can't come up with even one single plan."

"Me neither," I said. "But there is still some time. Maybe tomorrow a brilliant idea will turn up."

# Chapter 6

"This is the most wonderful day of my life!" I gazed adoringly at Enrique's back. He rode in front of me through a sunlit landscape surrounded by orange trees. Behind me came Rebecca on Duquesa, but I only had eyes for the handsome boy in front of me.

"I'm the lucky one," Enrique said. He turned around in the saddle to look at me. His glittering eyes make my heart skip. He liked me, I was sure of it. He didn't think I was too young. We came to a creek and I crossed it first, the other two following suit.

"What do you say about a canter when we get to that meadow over there?" I asked.

"What meadow? There aren't any meadows here," Enrique said. His voice sounded wooly and kind of distant, as if he was suddenly far away from me. How strange. I turned to look for him, but he was

gone. So was Rebecca. And the creek we had just crossed was gone as well. What was going on here?

Suddenly tall trees surrounded me. I had no idea where I was and I started to feel scared. But then, in front of me, I noticed a person. Relief flooded through me. Now I could ask for directions. I rode closer and closer . . .

Julio Merlota? What was he doing deep in the woods? Why was he just standing there staring at me? Now I was more frightened than before. Quickly I turned Evel to ride away.

"I've come to collect what's mine," Mr. Merlota called to me. His voice had a hollow, sinister sound. I didn't want to turn and look at him, but just then a high, ear-shattering noise filled the air and I wheeled Evel around to see what had made the sound. It was a horse and it whinnied again and again. San Silvo!

"No, you can't take him!" I screamed as Julio Merlota led San Silvo away. I wanted to ride after him, but suddenly Evel was gone and I was standing on the ground. Mr. Merlota started to run, San Silvo in tow.

"I can take whatever I want," Mr. Merlota shouted over his shoulder, "and you can't do a thing to stop me!"

He snapped his fingers and right before my eyes San Silvo began to shrink until he was no bigger than a miniature figurine. Mr. Merlota picked him up and put him into his pocket, laughing triumphantly. Thin, feeble whinnies were coming from his pocket.

"I told you that you were going to regret crossing me," he said. "Now do you believe meeeeee?"

I sat up, gasping for breath. For one confused moment I didn't know where I was, then it dawned on me. I was in my bed at the Quinta do Paraiso Alto, and it had all been a dream . . . a terrible nightmare. At least, the last part of the dream had been unpleasant. But I wish the first part could have been real, I thought as I settled down under my nice warm blanket again. There was daylight outside and birds were twittering. A glanced at the alarm clock told me it was 7:15. Time to get up. I heard sounds from the room next to mine and knew that Rebecca was up already.

As I crawled out of bed, stretching and yawning, I wondered if Paulina had managed to get any sleep. I doubted it. When Rebecca and I went to bed last night, she'd been in the living room, gulping down coffee, trying in vain to figure a way out of the problems. I hoped she was asleep now. She certainly needed it.

But when Rebecca and I entered the kitchen she was sitting there, morning paper in front of her. She didn't look as if she's slept at all. Her eyes were red and swollen, probably from crying. When she saw us, she hurriedly folded the newspaper. It didn't take a genius to know that she was trying to conceal it from us.

"Hi girls," she said, forcing herself to smile. "Are you up already?"

"Mmmm." Rebecca said, watching her mom closely. "Any exciting news in the paper today?" She nodded toward the rolled up paper that Paulina was now clasping to her chest.

Paulina shook her head. "Not really. I didn't finish it, though. I'll just take it with me and read the rest later."

She stood, walked quickly toward the door, and disappeared. Rebecca and I looked at each other. Then Rebecca turned and ran after her mom. When she returned a minute later, she was carrying the newspaper.

"I can understand why Mom wanted to spare us from seeing this!" Rebecca pointed at the article that filled most of the front page. "Just listen.

"Horse tormenter unmasked! Anonymous source blows the whistle. One of the most reputable horse breeders in the area is accused of seriously ill-treat-

ing her animals. Photo verifies horrifying cruelty . . .

Shock must have been written all over my face when I looked at Rebecca. A blurry photo that was supposed to be Paulina accompanied the article. Rebecca and I sank onto two of the kitchen chairs. We sat there for a long while, just gazing stupidly at each other. Then Rebecca said, "It says here that the photo that shows the abuse will be published in the evening paper. But how can they have proof? Mom has never beaten a horse in her life!"

"Maybe the person who says he's got the photo is bluffing and the newspaper people believe him." Even as I was saying the words, I could hear how stupid they sounded. No newspaper would publish something like that unless they knew they would be able to deliver the photo as promised.

"This is going to ruin us!" Rebecca's face was contorted with pain, and I saw tears in her eyes. "There must be something we can do!"

She looked at me expectantly, but my head was completely empty, except for a treacherous little suspicion that sneaked up on me, no matter how hard I tried to chase it away. If there really was a photo showing Paulina beating one of the horses, then it must be true, mustn't it? Maybe I didn't know Paulina as well as I thought. I tried to imagine her beating or whipping a horse, but I couldn't. No, I refused to believe that Paulina could mistreat a horse. I had to believe that she was innocent. I owed that to her, and to Rebecca. All the confusing thoughts racing through my mind made me sick.

"Come on, let's go feed the horses," I suggested, getting up from the table. "We won't solve anything by moping around here."

When we reached the stable yard, Paulina was just getting into her car. "I'm going to drive down to the newspaper office and demand to see the photo evidence they claim to have," she said. "They can't deny me that. I simply don't understand how they can have a photo showing me beating a horse. It's impossible. Completely impossible!"

She slammed the car door and drove off in a cloud of dust. Rebecca and I watched until it was out of sight.

"I hope Mom finds out it's all a huge mistake." Rebecca sighed. "Maybe they have a photo of someone resembling her . . ."

"Try not to worry too much," I said and gave her a hug. "I'm sure everything will be sorted out in the end. We know that Paulina is innocent, and somehow we're going to prove it!"

But did we really know she wasn't guilty? The treacherous little doubt reared its ugly head again. How could we be one

hundred percent sure? What if it was true? What if . . .

No, I refused to think more about this now. Rebecca and I were going to ride and just concentrate on the horses, and nothing but the horses, until Paulina came back. Maybe everything would be okay by then. But I knew I was only fooling myself. Nothing would be okay when she came back. I had a nagging feeling that she would be bringing us bad news – very bad news.

I looked toward the driveway. Was that a car coming? No, my ears must be playing tricks on me. The road was deserted; just as it had been the last time I glanced that way, no more than two minutes ago. Surely Paulina would come soon? It felt like we had been riding around in the paddock for ages. We were practicing jumps, but my mind wasn't on what I was doing, and of course Evel noticed. When I rode him toward a low parallel bar, one eye on the jump and one on the driveway, he nearly threw me off. At first he went obediently, preparing to jump, but at the last moment he shied and ran around the obstacle rather than jumping over it. Sheer luck stopped me from falling. I couldn't scold him. I knew perfectly well that it was my own fault.

"Sorry, I'm not myself today," I said, tousling his shiny mane. "I think we should put off jumping until my head is with me again."

"Just one more, then I'm done, too," Rebecca said. "And this time I'm going to get it right. Will you watch and tell me how I'm doing, Kimberly?"

"Sure," I said. "Go ahead."

Rebecca circled and steered Duquesa toward the parallel bar. They sailed over with inches to spare.

"Well done!" I tried to sound enthusiastic. "You leaned forward more that time."

"I could feel it the moment Duquesa took off," Rebecca said, pleased with herself. "This time we were in perfect balance. I've been struggling with this ever since I started jumping. It feels great to finally get it right."

"What do we do now?" I asked. "I really don't want to . . ."

Rebecca cut me short. "There's Mom," she said. "It's about time! I hope she's sorted out things with the newspaper, so they can print an apology in the evening paper."

We looked at Paulina expectantly when she got out of her car and hurried toward us. As soon as I saw her face, my worst fears were confirmed and I knew she didn't have good news for us. She looked flustered and she carried a sheet of paper. When she came closer, I saw that it was an enlarged photo.

"You might just as well see this right away," Paulina said gloomily. "It will be in the evening paper, and it will be the end of me! I can't imagine where this came from. It's just not right. I didn't do it, and yet this photo exists."

She held it up for us to see. I felt my entire body go cold. The photo showed Paulina using her whip on poor San Silvo. Blood was running down his side.

I looked at Paulina. So it was true after all, then! Almost without knowing what I was doing, I backed Evel a couple of steps away from her, as if I was afraid she would attack him as well. I closed my eyes and took a deep breath. I felt nauseous and the only clear thought in my mind was: I want to go home! I don't want to spend another minute here!

When I opened my eyes again, Paulina was standing there looking at me with a strange expression on her face. She looked almost – disappointed in me. But what could she expect?

"Kimberly," she said, her voice low. "You don't think that I did this horrible thing to San Silvo, do you?"

I glanced away, not knowing what to say. She had the evidence in her hand. How could she think I would believe that she was innocent?

Paulina sighed and her shoulders slumped. Without another word she spun around and walked toward the house. Rebecca hadn't said a word yet. I glanced at her, warily. She sat on Duquesa's back, as still as a statue. Her face was rigid, and she stared ahead of her with eyes that appeared to see nothing.

My heart contracted with pity.
It must have been horrible for
her to see her own mother
exposed this way. I wanted to
comfort her, but I didn't know
how.

# Chapter 7

"I don't believe it. I won't believe it!" Rebecca hid her face in her hands and burst into tears. "Mom would never do a thing like that. It can't be true!"

I had no idea what to say or do. Awkwardly, I put my hand on her shoulder. I wanted to tell her that everything was going to work out, but how could I, when disaster was just a few hours away? When the newspaper hit the streets, the whole district would get to see the despicable photo. Paulina might as well start packing immediately. She wouldn't be able to run the stud farm anymore. And neither should she, I thought indignantly. She ought to be kept away from horses forever.

"Hi." The familiar voice gave me a start. I'd been so lost in my own thoughts that I hadn't heard Enrique approaching. Now he stood there looking at us, a worried expression on his face.

Rebecca lifted her tear-stained face to him. "This is just too awful for words. Mom didn't do it, I know she didn't." Her voice rose. "You know Mom is innocent, don't you?"

Enrique hesitated and looked away. "I want to believe she is," he said slowly. "But I've seen the photo, and . . ." He shrugged, his voice trailing away.

"How can you let Mom down this way?" Rebecca asked, glaring at him. "And you, too, Kimberly! You think she's guilty, I can see it in your face. How could you? You of all people should know better!"

I still didn't know what to say. Rebecca's outburst was followed by a long, awkward silence. Enrique cleared his throat a couple of times as if he was going to say something, but in the end he just stroked Rebecca's hair and left. Rebecca and I sat and watched him go. When he disappeared around the corner, I sneaked a glance at my cousin. She wouldn't look at me. This was awful. I knew that if I said anything, no matter what, it would come out wrong.

Suddenly Rebecca stood, and without a word she stormed toward the house. When she reached the main entrance, she flung the door open and disappeared inside. I followed slowly, still with a huge lump in my throat. What on earth was I going to do?

Two hours had passed, and Rebecca was still in her room. I thought it would be best to leave her alone. I had no idea where Paulina was. In her office, most likely. After wandering restlessly from my room into the living room and back to my room again, I ended up outside, leafing through a magazine selling quality horse equipment. One full-page advertisement showed a well-equipped horse and his equally well outfitted rider balancing on the top of a mountain peak. "Our equipment brings you all the way to the top," the advert claimed.

Bah! I thought. What a stupid ad! Who, in their right mind, would like to balance on mountaintop like that? I knew it was supposed to symbolize reaching the top in competitions and all that, but I still thought the advert was too silly for words. I sat there glaring at the page as if the advertisement were to blame for all the unpleasant things that had happened since I came here.

The picture is a photomontage, they informed me in small letters at the bottom of the page. What a surprise, I thought sourly. Did they really think people were dumb enough to believe the photo was for real? As if a horse would ever be able to climb this high mountain . . . I shook my head, but stopped in mid-movement with a sharp intake of breath. I felt like someone had just emptied a bucket of ice water onto my head. I gaped at the image of the horse balancing so effortlessly on the mountain peak. Of course! I'd been such an idiot! Why didn't I think of this before? It changed everything!

"Rebecca!" I yelled at the top of my lungs. "Rebecca! Come on out here! Hurry! I've just discovered something!"

That I could have gone to her room instead of calling for her to come out didn't even enter my mind. My brain was reeling with the enormity of my discovery.

"What's up? You're screaming so loud they can probably hear you five miles away!" Rebecca was standing in the doorway looking at me. Her eyes were red and swollen, and the expression on her face told me that I was not her favorite person right now. But that was going to change.

I waved the magazine under her nose and told her what I'd come up with. Rebecca's face lit up. "You're right. Of course, this explains everything!" She grabbed the magazine and studied it closely. "The photo looks real, but it's a fake. Someone must have done the same thing with the picture of Mom. They've taken a regular picture and manipulated it until it looks like she's beating San Silvo half to death.

"But who could have done a thing like that, and how did they get hold of the photo in the first place?" I wondered.

"Getting it would be easy," Rebecca said. "The walls down at the Equestrian Society are plastered with pictures from various shows and events. There are lots of shots of Mom there. Anyone could just snatch a photo if they wanted to.

We looked at each other. "Julio Merlota!" we said simultaneously.

"I'm willing to bet you any amount of money that he's the person behind this," I added.

"I agree," Rebecca said eagerly. "No one has a better motive than that creep. He's green with envy because Mom is running the best stud farm in the district. Her ruin would be his gain. I'm sure that's what he thinks."

"To get Paulina through this mess in one piece, we have to expose him fast!" I said. "It's too late to do anything if she's already lost all her customers and gone bankrupt."

"Don't even say that!" Rebecca looked like she was going to burst into tears again. I felt like crying, myself, more from shame than anything else. How could I, even for a minute, have believed that

Paulina was capable of animal abuse? And Paulina knew what I'd been thinking. I felt sick remembering the look on her face. Would she ever forgive me? If Rebecca and I solved the photo mystery in time and cleared her name, she probably would. At least I hoped so.

Rebecca broke into my thoughts. "How are we going to prove that Mr. Merlota is behind all this?" she asked. "If we accuse him, he's just going to deny everything."

"I don't know," I said slowly.

Rebecca couldn't come up with anything useful either. "Let's go for a ride and think about it," she suggested at length. "Hanging around here without being able to help is driving me crazy!"

We had saddled the horses and were ready to go when Paulina came running toward us. I felt my face grow hot and I wondered if I should tell her how sorry I was, but I didn't get a chance to say anything. Paulina was carrying the photograph. Waving it in front of us, she said excitedly, "I've just discovered something really strange. This photo is impossible. It simply can't be real!"

"We know that it's not . . ." Rebecca began, but Paulina went on without taking any notice of her.

"The shirt I'm wearing in this photo was ruined when we cleaned out our old house before we moved here. I remember clearly throwing it in the garbage. At that time I had never so much as laid eyes on San Silvo. So how can I be with him in this photo, wearing clothes that I didn't even have anymore? I don't understand!"

"Don't worry, we do!" Rebecca said smugly.

Paulina looked at her. "What do you mean? What is it you two know that I don't?"

"It was Kimberly who figured it out." Rebecca answered.

I told Paulina about the advertisement I'd seen and that I'd realized how easy it would be for anyone to manipulate a photo, provided they had the right computer software and knew how to use it. "No doubt that's what happened in this case," I said eagerly, finally able to meet Paulina's eyes. "Someone put together at least two photos to make this one and then made it look like there was blood all over San Silvo's coat. And we think we know who did it."

"Julio Merlota!" Rebecca said. "We're sure he's behind this. Now all we have to do is prove it."

"But how are we going to do that?" Paulina glanced at the photo in her hand. "If Mr. Merlota is responsible for making this awful image, then I've a good mind to . . . to . . ." She clenched her hands into fist and stopped just short of saying what she'd like to do to Mr. Merlota. Maybe that was just as well.

"Couldn't you go down to the newspaper office and tell them the photo is a fake?" Rebecca asked her mom.

Paulina considered this, and then shook her head. "They'll just think it's a feeble attempt on my part to wriggle out of this mess. If I could bring proof that the photo is manipulated, it would be a different matter."

"We'll get hold of evidence," Rebecca stated. "Kimberly and I are going for a ride now to try figure out how."

"Good luck," Paulina said. "I'll try to come up with a solution, too. There has to be something we can do. I just wish I knew what. Maybe I should call the newspaper anyway. They probably won't listen to me, but I don't have anything to lose by trying."

Just then a brilliant idea popped into my head. I didn't mention it to Paulina, because I knew she'd never go along with it, not in a million years. I waited until Rebecca and I were well on our way. While the horses walked steadily along the broad riding track, I revealed my plan to her.

"Are you game for a little snooping?" I asked casually, and had to suppress a giggle when I saw her expression. "There is something I'd like to do. I want to check out Mr. Merlota's computer. To be able to manipulate the photo, he's got to have a program like Photoshop or something similar. We could try sneaking into his house and see what we can discover there. If we're really lucky, maybe we'll find

printouts of the pictures he sent to the newspaper."

"But how's that going to prove anything?" Rebecca looked at me, confused. "If we find printouts and take them with us he'll just deny he's ever seen them before."

"Fingerprints, for one thing!" I said triumphantly. "If the pictures are anywhere on his desk, it means he's touched them. If we can bring home printouts, Paulina can go to the police and they can check them for fingerprints, and boom! Game over for Mr. Merlota!"

"Good idea!" Rebecca grinned at me. "It's worth trying. But how are we going to get into his house without him seeing us?"

"We have to keep watch outside his farm until he leaves," I said. "Then we can sneak inside and see if we can find the evidence we need."

"I'm with you!" Rebecca exclaimed, eyes shining.

We rode on in silence for a while. Evel seemed to really enjoy his outing. I tried enjoying it, too, but the thought of what lay ahead of us, made my stomach knot. Breaking into Mr. Merlota's house. It was madness! What if he caught us? Would we end up in jail? I shuddered, having a vision of Rebecca and myself behind bars, crying for freedom. The image was so vivid that I almost turned Evel to ride home. But when I thought about Paulina and everything that was at stake, I changed my mind. We had to help her, no matter what!

All too soon we reached Mr. Merlota's farm. We steered the horses away from the track and into the woods. There we hid behind the trees, making sure we had a clear view of the road. If Mr. Merlota left in his car, we couldn't miss him. My heart was pounding in my chest and my mouth felt dry. My nervousness unsettled Evel, and he began pawing the ground and snorting excitedly. I leaned forward and patted his neck to calm him down. If he started whinnying now, it would blow our cover and ruin everything.

"Maybe that would be for the best," a little voice whispered in my ear. "What you plan to do is not just illegal; it's a serious crime. Turn around and leave while there's still time." I refused to listen to the voice. Stubbornly I kept on scratching Evel's mane and whispering softly to him.

The minutes crept by very slowly, and I began to feel impatient. "What if Mr. Merlota isn't going to leave the farm at all today?" I muttered to Rebecca. "What do we do then?"

"I'm sure he's going to go out today," Rebecca replied, keeping her voice low. "Mom said something about a meeting at the Equestrian Society, and Mr. Merlota is a member of the board, so he'll definitely be attending."

It turned out that Rebecca was right. Ten minutes later we heard a car door bang shut and an engine start. Mr. Merlota's dusty blue car came speeding down the road. The man obviously was no fan of safe driving, I thought, shaking my head. When the car was out of sight I turned to Rebecca, feeling a stab of anxiety in my chest. It was now or never!

Silently we rode down to the farm. Some of the buildings were just ruins, I saw. I vaguely remembered Paulina telling that he planned to tear them down. At the moment he was busy fixing up the stables. Not a moment too soon, I thought, shivering. There was a strange, spooky atmosphere around the place. I was glad we had come in broad daylight. Being here after dark would be creepy.

"Are there people somewhere on the property?" I whispered to Rebecca.

She nodded. "Mr. Merlota has a stablehand working for him," she said. "But Mom says he's too mean to have a housekeeper. We just have to stay clear of the stables, and we'll be fine."

"Okay," I said. "But what do we do with the horses? We can't just tether them and leave. They'd start whinnying like crazy."

"You stay here and watch them," Rebecca said. "And I'll sneak into the house and look for evidence."

"Wouldn't it be better if I went?" I felt I had to make the offer, even though the

thought of looking after the horses was much more appealing than tiptoeing around inside Mr. Merlota's house.

Rebecca shook her head. "It's my mom who's in trouble," she said. "And when she's in trouble, I'm in trouble, too. This is about saving our home! I should be the one to go inside."

Rebecca sounded so determined that I didn't protest. She handed me Duquesa's reins and walked swiftly to the nearest building. There she tried peeking in through a crack in the locked door. Did she suspect that someone might be inside? I dared not raise my voice to ask, in case the stablehand heard me. The next minute Rebecca disappeared around the corner, and I could do nothing but wait for her to return.

I spent the time whispering to the horses and patting them in turn to keep them quiet and calm. They kept tearing off mouthfuls of grass from the tufts growing close to the walls and seemed to enjoy the sun no end. Lucky horses, I thought. I was definitely not having a good time. My nerves were frayed. Why did the time have to pass so slowly? It felt like hours since Rebecca had disappeared, but my watch told me it was less than five minutes.

The sound of a car sent my heart up into my throat. Was Mr. Merlota coming back already? What should I do if it was him returning? No. The car drove past the farm. Relief turned my knees to water and I almost had to sit down. I grabbed Evel for support. Rebecca and I hadn't even discussed what to do if Mr. Merlota showed up while we were still here. If he did return, there was only one thing I could do – yell for Rebecca to get out of the house and ride for our lives. What Mr. Merlota would do if he found trespassers on his property, I didn't want to think about.

I was nearly out of my mind with worry when Rebecca finally showed up. She was empty-handed and didn't look happy. Without a word she grabbed Duquesa's reins and hoisted herself into the saddle. I followed suit, glad to be getting away from the place. Not until we'd crossed two farm roads and were back on the idyllic gravel road that led to Quinta do Paraiso Alto, did I open my mouth to speak.

"Did you find anything?" I asked, even though I knew the answer already.

She shook her head. "Not the things we wanted to find, that's for sure. But I did discover something . . ."

She broke off. I waited impatiently for her to continue.

"I looked everywhere in the house, and the only computer I found, was on a desk in his office."

"Yes?" I urged her on.

"It's the oldest clunker I've ever seen," Rebecca said. "It didn't even have a color screen. Maybe it has enough memory to run a simple word processing program, but that's about it. If anyone tried to install an advanced program like Photoshop in that ancient thing, it would probably fall to pieces from the shock!"

I just looked at her. "B-but then . . ." I stuttered. "Then he can't be . . ."

Rebecca shook her head. "Whoever manipulated that photo, Julio Merlota it was definitely not!"

# Chapter 8

"I've been thinking and pondering until my head spins!" I turned in the saddle to look at Rebecca. "And the more I think, the less I understand."

Rebecca and I hadn't said a word to each other for the last ten minutes. Now we were close to home and farther away from the truth than ever. At least it felt that way. We'd been so certain that Julio Merlota was the culprit that we'd never even considered other possibilities. Now I felt like the world's biggest idiot. In my mind I'd seen Rebecca and me coming home to Paulina, triumphantly bringing all the evidence that would restore her good reputation once and for all. Instead the only thing we had found out proved that Mr. Merlota was innocent. Or did it? Wasn't it possible that . . .

I'd just opened my mouth to speak, when a honk from behind startled me. We steered the horses onto the side of the road. For one horrible moment I was sure it was Mr. Merlota who had somehow found out that we'd been inside his house, and now he'd come after us to teach us a lesson. But when I turned my head, I saw it was not him.

The car slowed down, and Enrique popped his head out the open side window. "Hi girls," he said cheerfully. "Did you have a good ride?"

"Yeah, great!" I said, trying to sound enthusiastic. "Are you on your way to the city?"

Enrique nodded. "It's my day off," he said. "I'm visiting some friends. We'll probably go to the movies and maybe eat at a nice restaurant afterward. Anyway, I'm happy to get away from the stud farm for a few hours. The last days haven't been much fun." His face darkened. "I didn't expect this when I accepted the job," he muttered. "Everything seemed so great, but now . . ."

"It's much worse for my mom!" Rebecca said indignantly. "This could ruin her and then we'd have to leave the Quinta do Paraiso Alto. You can just get yourself another job or go back to your studies!"

"I'm sorry," Enrique said quickly. "I didn't mean to sound selfish. I do hope everything turns out in the end, although I can't see how Paulina is going to get out of this nightmare." He

shrugged, gave Rebecca an apologetic smile and drove off.

"He thinks Mom is guilty, that's easy to see," Rebecca said. "He doesn't say it straight out, since I'm her daughter, but thinks it just the same."

"Well, who can blame him? That horrible photo looks pretty convincing," I said, remembering with a stab of bad conscience that just a few hours ago I'd been convinced of Paulina's guilt, too. "We can talk to him tomorrow and tell him that the photo is a fake. And who knows, he may even be able to help us find the truth."

"What do you mean?" Rebecca looked at me.

"It dawned on me just before Enrique showed up," I said. "So what if Mr. Merlota has no proper computer equipment? That doesn't necessarily mean he's innocent. He could have an accomplice, someone who's helping him."

"But who?" Rebecca said.

I shrugged. "No idea. That's where Enrique could help us. He's made lots of contacts at the Equestrian Society. I'm sure he can find out if Mr. Merlota has a best buddy or something like that, someone willing to do his dirty work for him. Someone who's got a powerful desktop computer. At least it's worth a try, don't you think?

Rebecca nodded, but she didn't look very hopeful.

"Oh, look, aren't they cute?" Rebecca exclaimed, smiling and pointing at Evel and Duquesa. They stood facing each other, their muzzles touching, almost like they were sharing a friendly kiss. Looking at the two beautiful horses I felt warm inside, and for a few minutes I was able to forget the worries that hung over the stud farm. I just stood there admiring the two four-legged friends who were enjoying the beautiful day without a care in the world.

I lifted my face to the sun and smiled happily. When I phoned home an hour ago, Mom and I had talked about nice things only. I didn't mention Paulina's troubles, because that would make Mom sick with worry. What was the use of that? There was nothing she could do anyway. Just before we hung up, Mom told me that it was cold and rainy at home, which made me appreciate the sunny day even more.

My tiny bubble of happiness burst and I started pondering over the problems again. Apparently, Rebecca was doing the same, because as she grabbed for a grooming brush for Duquesa she said, "It makes me sick to think about how tongues are probably wagging all around the district now. I don't understand – how could the newspaper print the awful photo after Mom told them it was faked? Why didn't they believe her?"

"Maybe they did believe her," I said. "But maybe it didn't matter if they did."

Absentmindedly, I dragged the brush along Evel's back. It was a half-hearted attempt, but luckily, Evel didn't seem to notice. He had closed his eyes and was nodding his head, enjoying the brush and the warm sun equally. I stroked his muzzle. "You're the best," I told him. "You know that?" He nodded his head again, as if to say that he certainly did, but couldn't be bothered to open his eyes. "You lazy thing!" I patted his neck and continued grooming him.

"Why wouldn't it matter if they believed Mom or not?" Rebecca asked.

"Because dramatic headlines sell," I said. "I'll bet the evening paper is all sold out already. Did you notice the headline had a question mark and they called Paulina the alleged horse tormenter? That way the newspaper hasn't done anything wrong. They're just informing the public about the accusations against her. And if it's proven that she's innocent, then wham! The newspaper will have another sensational headline."

How Paulina was able to remain so calm when her life was falling to pieces around her was beyond me. "It's the way things work," she'd said, resignation in her voice. "The newspaper has a case and they write about it. I tried to stop them, but failed. I just have to live with that. There is nothing else I can do. But I'd sure like to get my hands on the person behind all this!"

We had told her about the unsuccessful expedition to Mr. Merlota's house, and she'd been appalled, but touched as well. "I probably should ground the two of you," she'd said, tears glistening in her eyes. "But I'm so proud of having two brave and resourceful girls like you on my side, that I'll let it pass for now. Just don't ever do anything like that again! What if Mr. Merlota had come home? Didn't you think about that?"

"We didn't think about anything else!" I giggled, feeling proud and embarrassed at the same time. How could Pauline praise me, when I'd suspected her along with everyone else? Quickly, I pushed the unpleasant thought away. "While Rebecca was inside the house, I almost had a nervous breakdown," I said. "And what's worse, it was all for nothing. But we still suspect that Mr. Merlota is guilty. Maybe he has an accomplice."

It was then Paulina told us something that made the case even more complicated. "I've been looking through my photo albums," she said. "In a couple of places there are pictures missing. I'm sure one the photos is of San Silvo. And the other one is from the time just before we moved. I remember that Rebecca and I fooled around with the camera while we were packing, so I guess that photo was of me."

"But don't you think Mr. Merlota could have sneaked in here and stolen the photos?" I asked.

Paulina shrugged. "Of course he could easily have gone inside the house without being detected," she said. "But I keep the albums on a shelf in my bedroom closet, so it would be a lucky hit for him to find them there . . ."

"Earth to Kimberly . . . earth to Kimberly . . . come in, please!"

"Huh?" I blinked in confusion as I was jerked back to reality. I'd been so deep in thought that I hadn't heard Rebecca trying to get my attention.

"How nice to have you back," she quipped. "Now that you're with us again, maybe you'd like to help me change the soiled straw with fresh bedding in Evel and Duquesa's stalls?" Rebecca said.

"Coming!" I said dutifully, getting my gear together.

"Phew! Cleaning out stalls is hard work. I'm glad we're finally finished!" Rebecca stretched her arms up in the air and took a few steps without noticing the dustbin that someone had left outside the stable door. She stubbed her toe hard and the bin overturned, spilling its contents. It had contained straw, paper and a variety of this and that, I observed.

"I guess you thought we needed some more work to do," I said sarcastically, as I bent to clean up the mess. That was when I noticed something that definitely didn't belong in the garbage.

Amazed, I picked it up to show Rebecca. "Look at this," I said. "I guess someone's going to be grateful you overturned that bin after all! I wonder who it belongs to?"

I opened the wallet and froze. "Rebecca," I squeaked. "You have a look too! Am I seeing things, or is this . . ."

"Good grief!" Rebecca reached out and touched the wallet lightly, as if she was afraid it might explode under her hand. "I don't understand."

But I did. Finally I understood everything! "Come on Rebecca!" I yelled excitedly. "We have to find Paulina. It's urgent!"

# Chapter 9

The stables were quiet and peaceful. Most of the horses were dozing in their stalls, well fed and content. A squeak from the stable door made a few of them prick their ears, but that was their only reaction. Had the visitor been a stranger, they might have been alarmed, but this was someone who sounded and smelled familiar. They were used to nightly visits like this, so they continued dozing peacefully. The new arrival didn't turn on the lights, but walked slowly from stall to stall, as silent as a shadow. When the form came to San Silvo's stall, it halted for a minute, regarding the handsome stallion. Suddenly, San Silvo became uneasy, sensing the hatred and envy that radiated toward him.

"Don't be afraid," the shadow whispered. "You're safe for now. But soon I'll be back, ready to fulfill my plan. Knock the last nail into the coffin, so to speak. And nobody will understand why this is happening. They never will! My plan is simple and brilliant, and soon – soon things will be as they should. She's got no one but herself to blame for what's going to happen. Why did she have to come here at all, pretending she owns this place? It's not fair! But I will make sure that justice is done. Soon she'll be gone. The door to victory stands open for me."

The large form gave a low, pleased giggle and left the stables. Once again it was silent. Only San Silvo remained uneasy. The stallion had a premonition that something evil was at large, planning to strike him, brutally and without mercy.

"Did you hear that?" Rebecca nudged my arm, making me jump. I'd been half asleep. The night had started with my being wide-awake, anticipating what was going to happen. But as the hours passed without incident, I grew more and more sleepy. When Rebecca suddenly heard something, I'd just dozed off.

I sat up straight, listening. Everything was quiet. Rebecca had to be wrong. But wait. Now I heard it too, the sound of footsteps closing in fast. My heart started hammering in my chest. We had planned this so well, but what if

anything went wrong? What if . . .?

The sound of the door handle being pushed down pulled me up short. The door opened and a dark shape stood silhouetted in the doorway. At the sight of Rebecca and me, it froze.

"What the . . ." he said, dumbfounded.

Enrique took a step toward us. His face showed a mix of confusion and growing anger. "What are you two doing here?"

"Waiting for you." Rebecca glared at him, sternly. "It's over, so you might as well confess!"

"Confess to what?" He looked totally bewildered. If I hadn't known better I might have believed he had no idea what we were talking about.

Enrique looked from Rebecca to me. "Is this supposed to be some kind of joke? Well, I'm not amused! And how did you get into my apartment? The door was locked, I know it."

"Paulina had extra keys," I said. "We borrowed them for a while."

"You have some nerve," Enrique spluttered. "You have no business being here. Get out immediately."

"Oh, but we have lots of business here," Rebecca said, holding up a photo for him to see. "Among other things, we were looking for some pictures. It was really stupid of you to keep the originals. You should have thrown them away as soon as you'd scanned them into the Mac we found in your bedroom."

"Have you been in my bedroom?" Enrique's eyes sparked with rage. Just then he looked nothing like the handsome guy who'd made my heart beat faster.

"We had to find evidence, didn't we?" Rebecca's smile was triumphant. "And did we ever! We found all we needed and more, both the original photos you used, and printouts of the manipulated photo you sent to the newspaper."

"I have no idea what you're talking about!" Enrique protested. "I've never seen these photos until now. Someone must have planted them in my room. Ah!" He pretended that something dawned on him. "Paulina! Of course! This must be some desperate attempt on her part to . . ."

"Don't even try," Paulina's voice floated in through the doorway. Enrique turned and saw her standing there, contempt written all over her face. "I've called the police and they're on the way, so why don't you just tell me the truth? To think that I liked and trusted you and now I discover that you're the one who's been giving me all this grief. How could you?"

"I tell you, I'm innocent!" Enrique tried to sound convincing, but his gaze flickered away from her. "Why would I try to harm you? Can't you see that your accusations are totally off the mark?"

"I'd say they hit the bull's eye, " Rebecca grinned. "You might as well give up, Enrique Sandor." Her smile broadened. "Or do you prefer that we use your real name, Enrique Merlota?"

"You shouldn't leave your wallet lying around for anyone to find," I added, handing it to him. "It gave us all the information we needed. Without it we'd never have sus-

pected you, because you don't look much like your uncle!"

"At least not on the outside," Paulina said. "But scratch the surface and you're both crooks. You've worked together to ruin me. Your plan could easily have succeeded if it hadn't been for my two wonderful, strong, intelligent, and resourceful girls!"

Enrique didn't say a word. He just snatched the wallet from my hand. For a moment he looked like he was tempted to push Paulina out of the way and make a run for it, but suddenly the sound of car tires could be heard on the gravel outside.

"The police have arrived," Paulina said. "Perfect timing!"

A short while later we watched as a subdued Enrique was led toward the police car and pushed into the back seat. The door slammed and that was the last we saw of him. While I watched them pull away, I thought about the crush I'd had on Enrique. He'd seemed so nice and friendly. It was so hard to believe it was all part of a plot he and his uncle had cooked up to destroy everything Paulina had worked so hard for.

"But he has ruined his own life and it serves him right!" I muttered under my breath, wondering if he regretted what he'd done. Probably not. Most likely he was just angry because his ingenious plans had failed.

I shrugged and followed Rebecca and Paulina out of the apartment. Now that all the excitement was over, I felt bone tired. I yawned so loudly it echoed in the corridor and Paulina laughed.

"Off to bed you go, girls," she said. "This has been a full day. I'll see you tomorrow and we can talk about what's happened. Right now I feel like I'm falling asleep on my feet. I haven't slept well lately. I have some catching up to do."

There were a lot of questions I wanted to ask. I still didn't know what Enrique had done to make San Silvo go berserk the way he did, but at this point I wasn't able to think straight. Paulina was right, there was no hurry anymore. We could talk tomorrow. I staggered into my room and didn't even bother to wash my face or brush my teeth. The last thing I remember is throwing my clothes on the floor and falling into bed. I think I was asleep before my head hit the pillow.

# Chapter 10

"Is Paulina still on the phone?" I sighed. "She promised we would talk today. There are still so many things I don't know."

Rebecca giggled. "Apparently everybody in the whole neighborhood is calling to apologize for believing Mom ill-treated San Silvo."

It was already past noon. Rebecca and I had slept until late morning and afterward we'd hung around the house and the stables waiting for Paulina to find time to talk with us. But so far we'd waited in vain. The news about Enrique being Julio Merlota's nephew from Lisbon had obviously spread like lightning and the phone had been ringing off the hook ever since.

"It's still difficult to believe that Enrique would do the things he did," Rebecca said, placing the saddle carefully on Duquesa's back. We were getting our horses ready for a ride. "He seemed so nice and he was great with the horses. How could he bring himself to hurt San Silvo? It's incredible!"

"I don't understand it either," I said, shaking my head. "And we still don't know what he did to torment San Silvo. The photo's one thing. I mean, the blood and everything was just faked on the computer and harmless to the horse. But those times at night in the stables . . . What do you think he did?"

"I'm not sure I want to know," Rebecca said. "And I can't stop thinking about the way he played up to Mom, all smiles and charm, making himself indispensable. And all the time he was working with Julio Merlota, plotting to force Mom into bankruptcy."

"It was a smart plan," I said, scratching Evel's forehead. He snorted contently, clipping his ears, as if he understood every word Rebecca and I were saying. But of course he didn't. He probably thought I was standing there praising him to high heaven.

"Sure, you're a fantastic horse. Isn't that what you wanted me to say?" I smiled, stroking his warm, velvety muzzle. Duquesa gave a loud, piercing whinny and stretched her head toward Evel, as if to say, "Don't imagine you're any better than I. It's me they should be praising!"

Evel didn't look overly impressed. I had to laugh. They were so incredibly cute.

The horses had been ready for a long time before Paulina finally appeared.

"Phew! My ear is all sore from being glued to the receiver all day," she said. "One more call and I'll go crazy. I've put on the answering machine and escaped."

"It's good that people at least have the decency to apologize for suspecting you," I said and felt another stab at my own conscience. I had suspected her, too, and I hadn't said I was sorry yet.

"They're not exactly apologizing," Paulina laughed. "Most of them are calling to tell me they didn't believe in the horrible rumors for a minute!"

"Do they really expect you to buy that?" Rebecca asked.

"I don't know what they're expecting," Paulina said. "But I guess it's their way of saying they're sorry, and that's fine with me. As long as I can get my life back on track, I'll accept any excuse, no matter how feeble!"

"Everything will be okay now, won't it?" I looked at her and she nodded.

"The truth is printed in today's paper and that is the end of it, once and for all."

"What about Julio Merlota?" Rebecca asked. "Was he arrested too?"

Paulina nodded. "I spoke with a police officer a while ago, and he told me they're both being interrogated now. He said they were tripping over their own feet to blame each other, so the family loyalty is starting to look rather frayed."

I giggled. "I hope they will have to share the same prison cell. Then they can pester each other instead of tormenting horses. Do you know now what they did to San Silvo?"

Paulina became serious. "According to the police officer, Enrique used plastic bags and electric shocks to scare San Silvo out of his wits. He'd sneak up on the horse flashing the bags. You know how spooked horses can be when unexpected things pop up from behind. And he

had this tiny device – a "stunner"', the officer called it. He used it to give San Silvo electric shocks. Not strong enough to be dangerous, but still very painful. He used the stunner the day we had the Open House as well, making it look like San Silvo was terrified of me.

I shivered. Enrique had to be evil to do a thing like that. But there was still something I didn't understand.

"I don't get it," I said to Paulina. "First Enrique and Julio put out rumors that San Silvo was crazy. Why did they do that if the whole point was to make people believe you were a horse tormenter?"

"The animal abuse thing was Enrique's idea," Paulina said. "He understood that his uncle was making a grave mistake by claiming that my prize stallion was going mad. Who'd want to cover their mares with a horse like that? San Silvo would have been useless to them, and Julio Merlota wouldn't have achieved a thing. So Enrique came up with a plan that would put me out of action without harming San Silvo's reputation. If he hadn't been a computer whiz, he'd probably never have thought of it."

Paulina stopped and looked around her. "When I think about how close he came to succeeding, I get cold all over. If I'd been forced to sell the Quinta do Paraiso Alto, I don't know what I would have done." She shuddered. "If it wasn't for you two . . ."

She looked at Rebecca and me. "I really love living here," she continued. "I haven't been this happy in years, not since . . ." Her words trailed away and I saw tears glistening in her eyes. I knew she was thinking about the time before the accident, when they'd still been a happy family of three.

Suddenly I had a huge lump in my throat and I burst into tears. I let go of Evel's reins and ran to Paulina. "I'm so sorry!" I wailed, throwing myself at her. "Will you ever be able to forgive me for suspecting you?" There, I'd finally said it. "Please, please forgive me! How could I ever, for one single second, think that you . . ." I broke off because I was crying so hard I couldn't say another word.

Paulina stroked my hair and gave me a hug. "You have nothing to feel sorry about. How could you not react? That photo was so convincing I almost began to suspect myself!"

"Thanks," I sniffled. "I don't deserve your kindness."

"Nonsense! It was you who discovered that the photo was faked. And even more important – it was you and Rebecca who found the evidence that exposed Enrique."

"But it was just luck that we found Enrique's wallet."

"What matters is that you did. Maybe it wasn't just luck. Maybe faith gave you a helping hand."

"If so, we're talking about a helping foot!" Rebecca giggled. "I stubbed my toe on the dustbin, remember? It's still sore."

"Forget all about the Merlotas for a while and go off on that ride," Paulina suggested. "Let the police handle them. Whatever happens next, they have no future here, that's for sure. And no horses either, for that matter. I heard that two local breeders are going to take over Mr. Merlota's stock."

"Good for the horses!" Rebecca said. "I'm sure they won't miss their horrible owner. I hope he and Enrique have the book thrown at them! They deserve everything they get!"

"I couldn't agree more! But off you go now, or I'll start thinking that you'd rather stay here and help out at the stables."

That got us moving. I swung myself onto Evel's back and soon we were on our way. When I passed the gate that led to the gravel road, I turned to look back. Paulina was heading for the stables, her steps eager and springy. She seemed ten years younger than yesterday. I was so happy for her. Now she and Rebecca could go on living in security at the farm. And I'd helped make it possible. That felt really good.

# Epilogue

"My last day here! I can't believe how fast the time has flown by!"

"And what a time!" Rebecca laughed. "You sure can't say that your stay here has been boring!"

I shook my head, grinning. "This has been the most dramatic week in my whole life. And even though it ended happily, I hope I'll never experience anything like this ever again. But the last couple of days have been great, just like I dreamed they would be when I came here."

I felt a painful sting in my chest when I realized that this was my last ride on Evel. I slowed him down to a halt and looked at Rebecca. "If my face turns all green, it's not because I'm feeling sick or anything."

Rebecca just stared at me, not understanding what I was talking about.

"I'm envious, you twit!" I said, trying to ignore the big lump in my throat. "Tomorrow I'll be back in cold Vermont again, while you're still here, enjoying the lovely spring weather, surrounded by beautiful horses. Soon the foals will be born, and I won't be here to see them and . . ."

Tears stung my eyes and I got really upset when Rebecca just laughed. How could she be so insensitive?

"You think this is funny?" I said, shooting daggers at her with my eyes. Not an easy task when you're struggling not to cry. I failed miserably. "It isn't funny, just so you know!"

"But you will get to see the foals! Didn't Mom tell you? She's hopeless!" Rebecca shook her head.

"What do you mean?" It was my turn to stare at her.

"To make a short story long, or is it the other way around?" Rebecca teased, but I didn't swallow the bait to try and correct her English this time. I just waited for her to explain.

"Okay," Rebecca said. "I'll tell you. Yesterday my mom called your mom, who then called your dad, and everything was settled."

"What's settled? You're talking in riddles." I felt like shaking her, because she was keeping me in suspense on purpose. She was enjoying every second of it.

"The summer vacation, of course!" Rebecca said, as if I should have known.

"What about it?" I felt my heart starting to beat faster.

"You're staying with us!" Rebecca was smiling from ear to ear now. "Well, your parents will only be here for two weeks, but you can stay the whole vacation if you like."

Stay here at the Quinta do Paraiso Alto the whole summer vacation? Be with Rebecca every day? Play with the little foals? Ride Evel as often as I wanted?

"Hurray!" I yelled, startling poor Evel. He whinnied in protest and tossed his head.

"Sorry, I didn't mean to scare you. " I leaned forward to scratch his neck. Evel snorted and I could almost hear him saying, "Hey, you better behave. Shrill noises like this are not to my liking, thank you very much!"

"Should I take that as as yes?" Rebecca asked.

"Since you're obviously very slow at the uptake, I'll feed it to you with tiny little tea-spoons," I said. "Yes, thank you, I'd love to stay here the whole summer vacation. You didn't doubt that, did you?"

"Well, not really," Rebecca said happily. "Oh, Kimberly, we're going to have so much fun, at least most of the time. I

guess we're going to have to help Mom at the stables as well. She's advertising for a new stablehand, of course, but still . . ."

"I don't mind helping out at the stables," I said. The lump in my throat was completely gone.

"I'm looking forward to the vacation already," Rebecca said.

"Me too! We can E-mail each other and make heaps of plans about what we're going to do, and we can . . ."

"We can start by enjoying this day!" Rebecca interrupted.

"We will!" I smiled at my cousin. Now that I knew I was coming back here, I wanted to sing out loud. But my singing has always been best kept private, so out of consideration for the horses, I kept quiet.

While Evel trotted calmly along the soft trail, I started counting how many days I had to wait for summer vacation to start. It really wasn't that many, I happily realized. And this vacation was going to be the best of my life, I was already sure of it.

Thanks to Jinny Harman for assisting us and letting us use her horses and stables, and to our two-legged models Camilla Jamesson, Rebecca Mangan, Rupert Harman, Paula Barros and Rui Nuno, and to our four-legged, patient models Dutchess, Vagabond and Evel.